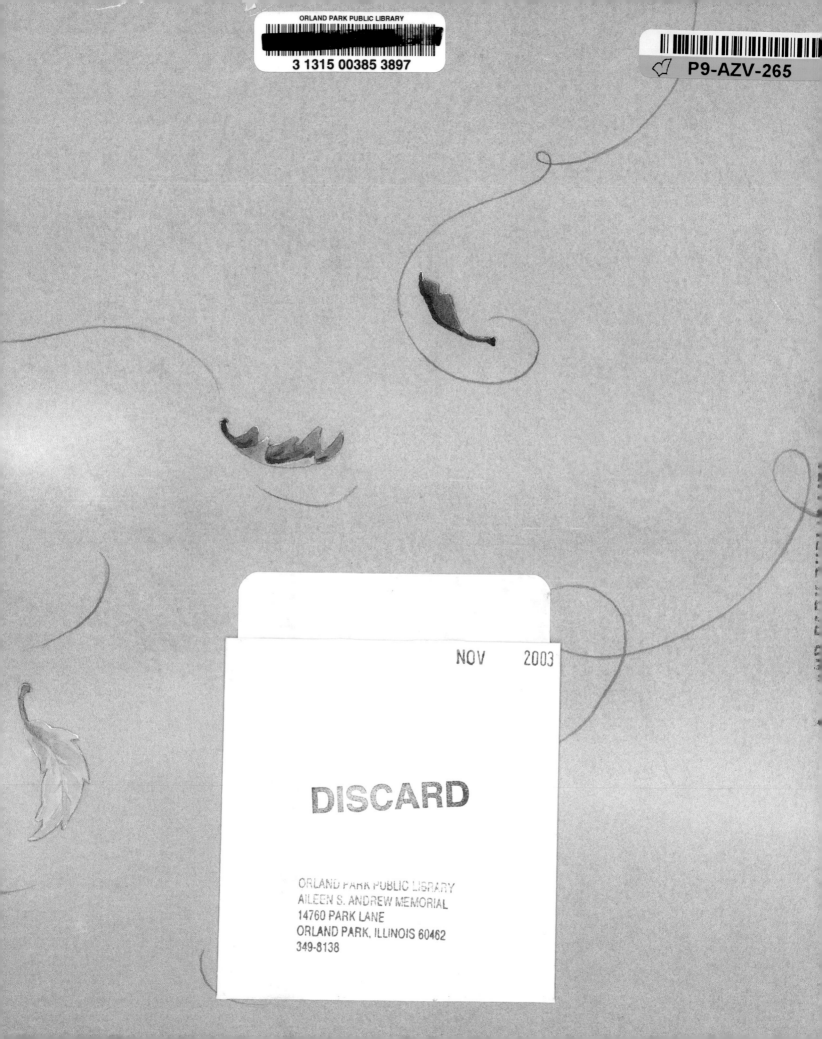

For Joan, my writing buddy
—CF.

For Alex Abbey
—VC

tiger tales
an imprint of ME Media, LLC
202 Old Ridgefield Road, Wilton, CT 06897
Published in the United States 2003
Originally published in Great Britain 2003 by Little Tiger Press
An imprint of Magi Publications
Text copyright ©2003 Claire Freedman
Illustrations copyright ©2003 Vanessa Cabban
CIP data is available
ISBN 1-58925-030-3
Printed in Italy
All rights reserved
1 3 5 7 9 10 8 6 4 2

Gooseberry Goose

by Claire Freedman

Illustrated by
Vanessa Cabban

tiger tales

The sun was up and shining. Red and gold leaves fell from the trees. "Wake up little Gooseberry!" called Mama Goose. "It's lovely weather for you to practice flying."

"Yippee!" said Gooseberry, jumping out of bed.

After breakfast, Gooseberry flapped through the fallen leaves all the way to the lake. His friend Beaver was there, working in the water and swimming around.

"Hey Beaver!" called out Gooseberry. "Do you want to watch me taking off and landing?"

Gooseberry ran as fast as he could along the shore. "Clear the runway!" he shouted. "Vrooooom!" He soared right over Beaver's head and landed with a bump.

"Did you see that?" Gooseberry asked Beaver.
"I'm getting better and better every day."

"Great landing," said Beaver. "But I'm sorry
I can't stop working, Gooseberry. I have to finish
building my dam before winter comes." And with a
wave of his paw, Beaver disappeared below the water.

Gooseberry zig-zagged through the air, backward and forward across the lake. Orange and yellow leaves fell from the trees. "I bet I can float through the air like the leaves do," said Gooseberry. He decided to try it.

"Up, up, and away!" shouted Gooseberry.
"Whooooosh!"
      It wasn't that easy. But someone was
clapping for Gooseberry!

"Great flying," called out Squirrel.

"Watch me do it again!" said Gooseberry. "I can glide on the wind!"

"I'm sorry Gooseberry, but I have a lot of work to do," said Squirrel. "I'm busy finding food and hiding it for winter." Squirrel scampered away to bury his acorns.

As Gooseberry practiced his swoops and dives, he spotted his friend Mouse. "Look at my loop-the-loops, Mouse!" he called. "I've been practicing all morning!"

"That's great, Gooseberry!" said Mouse. "I can't stay and watch, though. I have to find something warm to make my nest with. Haven't you heard?"

"Yes, I know," said Gooseberry. "Winter is coming, and everyone's busy."

"You should really start getting ready for winter, too," said Mouse before she scurried off.

"Maybe Mouse is right," thought Gooseberry. "But I don't know how to get ready for winter." Gooseberry thought he should look for berries and seeds to save, but it was hard work. "Ugh! I'd rather practice flying!"

Fluffy white clouds swirled through the blue sky.
"I wonder how high I can fly?" thought Gooseberry.
Up, up, up he soared, and down, down, down he glided.
"Whee!" cried Gooseberry. "I've never done that before!"
  "That looks scary!" called out Rabbit, who was
watching from the ground.

"Did you see how high I went?" said Gooseberry. "I can show you again, if you'd like."

"Well, I'd like to, but I'm working very hard right now," said Rabbit. "I have to clean out my den and make it cozy before winter comes." And Rabbit quickly hopped down his hole.

Suddenly a chilly little breeze ruffled Gooseberry's feathers. He began to feel a little bit worried. Winter was coming! Everyone was getting ready except him. Gooseberry thought he should hurry up and do something about it. He flew back home in a hurry.

"What's the matter, Gooseberry?" asked Mama when she saw him hurrying home.

"Winter's coming! And I'm not ready!" said Gooseberry.

Mama laughed. "Little Gooseberry, don't you remember what I told you? Geese don't stay here for the winter. It gets too cold!"

"We'll be flying south, where it will be nice and warm," Papa said. "It's a long, long trip, and that's why you needed to practice flying. You've been getting ready for winter all day!"

"I guess I have been all along!" said Gooseberry. "I bet I can fly for miles and miles. Watch me fly!" And Gooseberry dove and soared and glided in the fading blue sky, just like the red and gold leaves that floated down from the trees.